For
Caitlin
in the King's CHAIR
and for N.D.W.

A Maple TREE Begins

WRITTEN & ILLUSTRATED BY

Aldren A. Watson

NEW YORK

THE VIKING PRESS

CAITLIN stood at the window in the front hall, watching the sap buckets swinging in the wind. They rolled against the tree trunks, their flat lids flapping and clattering. Fine grains of drifting March snow sifted through the crack under the big front door, and the dried branches of a bush scratched like birds' feet on a windowpane.

Leif, Peter's big German shepherd, sat on the hall rug and moaned softly.

"It's all right, Leif," said Caitlin, sitting down beside him and stroking his head. "Peter will be home from college soon." Leif pricked up his ears and looked toward the door.

Suddenly there was a sharp crack like a great bone snapping, then a roar as from a great wind, then *boom*! The whole house shook and the windows rattled in their frames.

Caitlin rushed to the window. "Mom!" she shouted. "Come quick! The whole tree fell down!"

"Cait, are you all right?" her mother called from the kitchen. "What happened?"

"The big maple tree crashed down in the wind!" Caitlin said.

They stood together at the window and looked out. Up where the branches had waved against the sky there was nothing, just empty blue and the barren hill beyond. The giant, gray-barked tree lay broken in the snow. Where the tree had cracked off, long splinters of wood shimmered wet and yellow in the morning sun. Part of the center of the stump was filled with brown, crumbly rot. The biggest limbs held the tree off the ground a little, but the smaller branches were doubled back and tangled in crazy ways under the great weight. The wind swept and pulled at them as if trying to straighten them into life again.

"The old tree is dead now," Caitlin said sadly.

"Yes," said her mother. "It must have been very old."

"How old?" asked Caitlin.

"I have an idea," said her mother, "that the trees were planted in the yard at the same time this house was built. That was during the Revolutionary War."

"Is the tree *that* old?" Caitlin asked.

"There's a way to tell," said her mother. "When Peter comes home this morning, ask him how to tell the age of the tree. He'll know."

The first thing Peter said when he came in was, "When did the big tree go down?"

Caitlin told him the whole story. Then she asked, "How old is the tree, Peter? Can you tell? Is it as old as Mother said?"

"Let's go out and take a look," said Peter, giving her a hug.

They got the chain saw from the shed and carried it around to the front of the house. Peter yanked the starting rope several times and suddenly the saw started, sending a cloud of blue smoke into the cold air. Soon it was running smoothly, making a deafening roar.

Peter looked at the ragged end of the tree trunk, measuring off by eye where to make the first cut. He picked up the saw and laid the blade against the bark. Then he squeezed the throttle. The saw whined into a high-pitched song, biting into the wood and showering yellow sawdust onto the snow. Down and down into the thick trunk the saw ate, until finally it came through on the underside. The big, ragged butt of the tree fell heavily to the ground.

"There," said Peter, shutting off the saw. "Now you can see for yourself how old it is."

"How?" asked Caitlin.

Peter knelt in the snow and wiped the sawdust from the cut end of the tree trunk. "See those rings in the wood? You have to look hard, because the chain saw leaves the wood rough."

Caitlin peered at the sawn end of the tree. "Now I see them," she said. "What do the rings mean?"

"Every year the tree lives, it adds another ring to its wood. By counting the rings, you can tell how old the tree is."

"How does it do that?" asked Caitlin, frowning.

"By growing in a certain rhythm," said Peter. "In early spring the sugar maple grows very fast. Fast growth makes big, thin-walled cells, and they are light-colored. After June it grows very

slowly, and slow growth makes smaller, thicker-walled cells that are dark-colored. The difference in color between the spring wood and the summer wood makes annual rings show up."

Caitlin looked puzzled. "But doesn't the tree grow all the time?"

"No," said Peter, "it isn't like you, eating and sleeping and growing all summer and all winter too. In winter the sugar maple lies dormant—it's asleep. When spring weather comes and warms the sap, the tree bursts into growth again. Then in summer it slows down and you get another annual ring."

"How can it grow if it doesn't eat?" asked Caitlin.

"Speaking of eating," Peter said with a grin, "let's get some lunch. I'll make a drawing to show you how the maple tree begins."

They went inside and Peter got out a drawing pad while Caitlin made them each a sandwich. Then she climbed into a chair and watched Peter draw.

bark

sapwood

heartwood

Annual rings make the "grain" in boards.

Seed and wing is called "key."

The two keys very often break apart and fly away separately.

"These are maple seeds, Cait. Every three or four years a huge crop of seeds appears on the big, grown-up maples like the one that fell down. In late summer, before the leaves fall off, the seeds ripen and drop. Each tree sheds hundreds and hundreds of seeds. They come in pairs, with a little wing on either side."

"What are the wings for, flying?" asked Caitlin.

"That's right," said Peter. "The wings make the seeds twirl and spin as they fall. The wind catches them and blows them along, so they'll spin out into the forest and start trees in new places. If they didn't have wings, all the seeds would fall straight down and land right under the parent tree. They would start to grow there, but they wouldn't have room to grow big and tall. The wings give the seeds a way of moving to new places where there is plenty of space for them to grow properly and become mature trees."

"When the seed falls, does it start to grow a new little tree right away?" asked Caitlin.

"Think a minute," said Peter. "It's autumn when the seed drops. What would happen if a tender new plant started to grow just before snow falls?"

"It would die of the cold," said Caitlin.

Keys twirl
and spiral as they fall.

15

"Yes," said Peter. "So the seed doesn't put out anything above the ground that first autumn. It lies on the ground and is covered by the leaves that fall from the trees. Then it waits for cold weather and snow."

"Don't the ice and snow hurt the seed?"

"No, it has a hard, dry coat to protect it. In fact, the sugar maple seed won't even start to grow until after it has had that kind of cold treatment. I guess that's nature's way of making sure the seeds won't germinate until spring, when a baby tree has a good chance to live."

"What does 'germinate' mean?" Caitlin asked.

"That's what happens in the spring. Sometime in April the snow melts and the sun warms the earth. The seed coat bursts and a tiny shoot pokes its way up through the earth and dead leaves and dried grass toward the sunlight. At the same time, a little root begins to grow down into the earth, to anchor the new seedling to the ground, and to get water and minerals for making its food. So you see, Caity, the tree does need food to grow, just as you do."

"Does the seedling look like a maple tree?" asked Caitlin.

"Not really," said Peter, "not yet. After the shoot struggles up through the clutter of dead leaves, the seed coat splits still more and two little seed leaves unfold. Between these two leaves is the growing point of the tree. Then it looks like this."

Peter drew for a minute. "The two first leaves are called *cotyledons* and they don't look much like maple leaves. They're long and narrow and hang down sort of limply. They aren't shaped like a regular leaf from an adult maple tree. And they

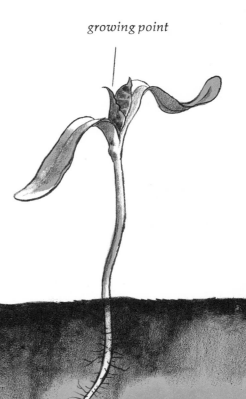

growing point

seed leaves, or cotyledons

17

are quite red, not green as you would expect." He put the finishing touches on his drawing and pushed it over for Caitlin to see.

"You mean the big maple tree started out like *that*, with those funny little strips of leaves?" Caitlin said.

Peter nodded. "Hard to believe, isn't it?"

"Then what happens?" asked Caitlin.

"The seedling starts growing taller and puts out two primary leaves. But they aren't like maple leaves either; they're oval and pointed. Only then do the regular square maple leaves appear— four or five pairs growing from the tip of the little stem. In between each pair of leaves the stem gets longer. By June it has all the leaves it'll get that first year. Then it just about stops growing taller, though the stem may get a little bigger around before fall."

growing point

primary leaves

first true maple leaves

primary leaves

cotyledons

"Does it just sit there and do nothing the rest of the summer?" Caitlin asked.

"No, it spends the rest of the summer getting ready for winter, just the way bees and squirrels and farmers do. In July it makes new buds at the tip of the stem and also along the length of the stem where the leaves are attached. And it stores up energy in the form of sugary sap, to use for the tremendous burst of growth it will make again the following spring."

"Where does the tree store its food?" Caitlin asked. "It has no beehive and no pantry!"

"It stores the sap in the wood underneath the bark, where it stays all winter until the tree needs it for new growth in the spring."

"Or until we steal it to make maple syrup!" said Caitlin. "What does it do after it makes the buds and stores the sap?"

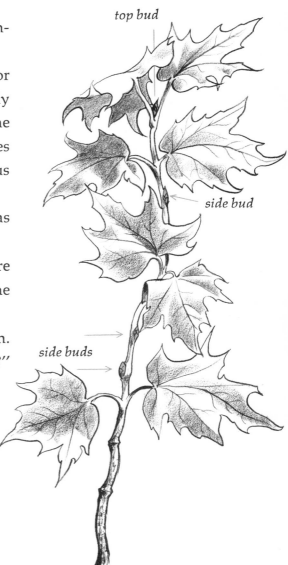

top bud

side bud

side buds

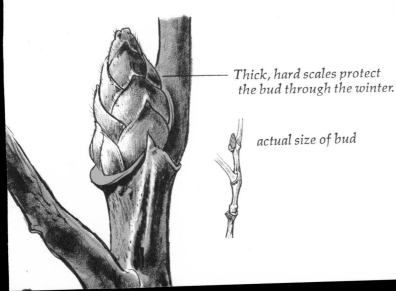

Thick, hard scales protect the bud through the winter.

actual size of bud

two-year seedling
7 inches high

five years
30 inches high

ten years
12 feet high

20

"Then," said Peter, "autumn comes. The nights get long and the air gets cold. The leaves turn beautiful shades of red and yellow, dry up, and drop off. The tree stops all its activity and goes dormant again.

"The next spring there's another great burst of growth, with new sets of leaves and branches growing from the buds it made the summer before. The seedling begins to look like a real tree. And so it grows, year after year. When the tree is thirty or forty years old, it will flower and produce its first crop of seeds and drop them to make its own new seedlings."

"Peter, do you really think the old tree goes back to the Revolutionary War? That's really old!"

"Not so old for a maple tree," said Peter. "They can live to be three or four hundred years old. Wouldn't it be fun to find out what was going on in the world when the tree was just a sprout?"

"Yes," said Caitlin, "and how old it was when exciting things happened!"

"All right, let's make a calendar on the tree," Peter said.

They got pencils, paper, and thumbtacks, and went outside.

"First let's find out how old the tree was." Peter scraped and

21

Lewis & Clark   Civil War   Klondike   Lindbergh   Caitlin   Tree fell

smoothed part of the wood with his knife. "You count the rings from your side to the center and I'll do the same from my side. Make a pencil mark every tenth ring so you won't lose track."

They counted busily for a while. Then Caitlin looked up. "I've finished, Peter. I have nineteen pencil marks and four rings left over. How many did you get?"

"The same. That means the tree is about one hundred ninety-four years old. The seed could have hit the ground the summer they signed the Declaration of Independence. How about that!"

Peter wrote a tag that said July 4, 1776, and with a thumbtack pinned it to the center of the tree. "All right, Caity, what shall we put on next?"

"Lewis and Clark Expedition, 1803. And the Civil War, 1861, all right? Can I make the tags?"

Caitlin made the tags and tacked them in place. "I can't think of anything else," she said.

"There was the Klondike gold rush in 1896," said Peter, "and in 1927 Lindbergh flew alone from New York to Paris."

"Good," said Caitlin, "but we need something for just before the tree died. Didn't anything exciting happen after Lindbergh?"

"Sure," said Peter. "You were born!"

Caitlin laughed, and they tacked up all the tags.

"I wish I could take the tree to school with all the tags on it," she said. "That would make a good history report, wouldn't it?"

"Cait!" said Peter suddenly. "Look at the spout still sticking in the tree! It's dripping sap!"

Caitlin looked behind her. Sure enough, a spout which had held a sap bucket that windy morning was still stuck in the fallen tree, and sap was dripping slowly from its tip. Caitlin ran to it and knelt down to catch the drip on her tongue. "Oh, good!" she said.

"I guess we'll never make syrup again from this tree," Peter said.

Caitlin sat back on her heels and thought a minute. "Peter," she said, "what's going to happen to the tree now?"

"Firewood," said Peter. "There's enough in this tree to last us half the winter."

"Poor tree," said Caitlin.

"No, Cait, it's a wonderful tree. The old people call a tree like this 'twice-warming wood.' It warms you once when you cut it, and again when you burn it!"

Caitlin laughed. Then she said, "Can we cut it all up for the fireplace before you have to go back to college?"

"We can try," said Peter.

Next morning the woodcutting began. For several days Peter

and Caitlin worked at the big tree. Peter started by chopping off the top branches with the ax and working them up into short sticks that would fit in the fireplace. Nearer the base of the tree the limbs and branches were too thick for the ax, and he had to use the chain saw.

At last the great bole lay on the ground, cleaned of all its branches. Then Peter started on the main trunk. He sawed off big blocks and used the ax to split them into smaller chunks. Every time the ax came down on the end of a block, it made a sharp popping sound in the cold air.

"Look at the sap squirt out!" cried Caitlin.

As Peter split the wood, Caitlin loaded it onto the toboggan and pulled it around to the woodshed. Each time she went back for another load, the tree was a little smaller.

Finally every stick of wood was in the shed. The only trace of the tree was a long, ragged hollow in the snow, and piles and piles of sawdust. But the woodshed looked beautiful, neatly stacked high with bright new logs.

When Peter's spring vacation was over, he left to go back to college. Caitlin was lonely at first. Every day the spring air was a bit warmer, and she watched the big maples turn a deep, rich green as their leaves opened and spread. In the front yard where the old sugar maple had stood, there was a big hole through the treetops showing a bright patch of blue sky. The yard looked different, too. It was bare and empty where the big tree had rested. The stump remained, though, and Caitlin could climb into the part where the crumbly rot had been. It's like a jagged old king's chair, she thought.

One day as she sat in the king's chair she discovered something. In a hollow beside the stump a tiny maple seedling was poking up through the carpet of last year's leaves. Its spindly stem was all speckled with tiny yellow spots, and at the tip were two pale reddish leaves. They were crinkled and creased, hanging limply from the tip of the new little tree.

Caitlin sat and watched for a long time. It was as if the old maple wasn't really dead after all. For the new one was growing right where the old tree had stood, from a seed it had dropped in its last year.

Caitlin smiled. "When Peter comes home again, that's the very first thing I'll show him."

INDEX

Page numbers in italics refer to illustrations.